Lisa
the Jelly Bean Fairy

by Daisy Meadows

ORCHARD

www.rainbowmagic.co.uk

Jack Frost's Spell

Give me candy! Give me sweets!
Give me sticky, fizzy treats!
Lollipops and fudge so yummy -
Bring them here to fill my tummy.

Monica, I'll steal from you.
Gabby, Lisa, Shelley too.
I will build a sweetie shop,
So I can eat until I pop!

Contents

Surprises

"This is a bumpy ride!" said Kirsty Tate
with a laugh.

She and her best friend Rachel Walker
giggled as they bounced up and down.
Kirsty's Aunt Harri patted the dashboard.

"I love this good old Candy Land van,"
she said. "Even if it is a bit noisy and
bumpy sometimes."

Candy Land was the sweet factory just outside Wetherbury Village, and Aunt Harri was lucky enough to work there.

"Candy Land is my second favourite thing about Wetherbury," said Rachel.

"What's your favourite?" asked Kirsty.

"Staying with you, of course," said Rachel with a grin. "It's always magical."

Rachel had come to visit Kirsty for the school holidays. Ever since they had become best friends, they had also been good friends with the fairies. Magic always seemed to follow them around when they were together. Sometimes they thought that it was as if their friendship cast a very special spell.

This time, Monica the Marshmallow Fairy had whisked them away to the Fairyland Sweet Factory, where sweets grew on trees. They had met the other Candy Land Fairies, who used their magical objects to make sure that all candy was sweet and delicious. The fairies were getting ready for the annual

Harvest Feast, and asked Rachel and
Kirsty if they would like to come. But
just then, Jack Frost had appeared with
his goblins. He had stolen the Candy
Land Fairies' magical objects so that he
could keep all sweets for himself.

Kirsty and Rachel had helped two
of the Candy Land Fairies to get their
magical objects back, but there were still
two more to find. However, today they
had something else on their minds. They
were on their way to see a boy called Tal,
who volunteered as a dog walker at the
Wetherbury Animal Shelter.

"I can't wait to see Tal's face when he
finds out that he's a winner," said Kirsty.

Candy Land had been giving its
Helping Hands Awards to young people
who did helpful things in the community.

The girls had been helping Aunt Harri to surprise the winners with special bags of Candy Land treats.

"What's inside Tal's Candy Land bag?" Rachel asked.

"Jelly beans," said Aunt Harri, smiling.

"Yum, I love jelly beans," said Kirsty.

"I brought along a small packet of them for you to share," said Aunt Harri. "You'll find them in the back of my seat."

Rachel put her hand into the little pocket on the back of Aunt Harri's seat, and found the packet. She opened it and chose a purple one.

"Grape flavour is my favourite," she said, holding out the bag to Kirsty.

"Mine's strawberry," said Kirsty, choosing a pink one. "Thank you so much, Aunt Harri!"

Just then, Aunt Harri turned down a narrow, rutted lane. Kirsty squealed as the van went over a big bump in the road, shaking and rattling. It was even noisier than before. Smiling, the girls popped the sweets into their mouths. But when they

tasted them, they got a terrible shock.

"Ugh," said Rachel.

"Yuck," said Kirsty.

Rachel pulled a tissue out of her pocket and both girls put the jelly beans into it.

"That wasn't strawberry flavour," said Kirsty. "It tasted like sour milk."

"Mine was like rotten eggs," said

Rachel. "Oh no, what if Tal's jelly beans taste bad too?"

"They're bound to," said Kirsty. "Oh dear, this is all Jack Frost's fault."

They exchanged a worried look and then glanced at Aunt Harri. Because of the noisy van, she hadn't heard anything. And that was lucky, because the girls had promised never to tell anyone about Fairyland or the fairies.

Rachel and Kirsty knew exactly what was wrong with the jelly beans. The Candy Land Fairies were still missing two of their magical sweets. Without them, the Harvest Feast would be ruined, and so would Tal's bag of jelly beans.

Suddenly, Kirsty noticed something unusual. The Helping Hands bag was glowing. The pink and white stripes

shone as if each jelly bean inside the bag was a tiny light.

"That's magic," Kirsty whispered in excitement.

Rachel's heart was fluttering. No matter how many times she shared magical adventures with her best friend, every time was always just as thrilling as their very first meeting with the fairies on Rainspell Island.

Smiling, she opened the bag, and out
flew Lisa the Jelly Bean Fairy.

Three Thieves

Lisa flashed a dazzling smile at the girls. Then she fluttered behind Aunt Harri's seat so that she couldn't be seen from the front of the car.

"It's good to see you both," she said. "I heard you talking about how awful your sweets tasted. I'm so sorry! It's because Jack Frost and the goblins have my

magical jelly bean. I want to get it back, but I don't know where to start looking. Will you help me?"

"Of course we will," said Rachel in a low, determined voice.

She glanced at Aunt Harri. Luckily
the noise of the van was so loud that she
hadn't noticed a thing.

"We're almost at the animal shelter,"
said Kirsty. "You'll have to be as quick
as possible, Lisa."

Hastily, she opened
her rucksack and
let Lisa flutter
inside. Aunt Harri
parked the van
and the girls
climbed out.

The animal shelter
was a long, low building.
Around it, green hills rolled away in
all directions. Aunt Harri led the girls
towards the front door. Inside, the first
thing the girls noticed was a giant jar

of jelly beans on the reception counter.
While Aunt Harri went to speak to the
receptionist, Rachel and Kirsty went to
look at the jar. There was a sign propped
up beside it.

Raise money for the animal shelter and win a
month's supply of pet food!
Guess how many jelly beans are in the jar.
Tell the receptionist your guess!

"We're here to give Tal a Candy Land's
Helping Hands Award," Aunt Harri told
the receptionist.

The receptionist was wearing a name
badge that said 'JB', and he gave Aunt

Harri a wide grin.

"That's great news," he said. "Tal's a real star around here. All the animals love him – he's even organised this competition to raise money."

"Candy Land was really impressed when we heard about Tal's work for the shelter," said Aunt Harri. "We've got a very big bag of sweets for him."

"He's taken two of the dogs out for a walk," said JB. "He'll be back soon. You can wait for him here in reception if you like."

Just then, there was a volley of barks from the back of the shelter and JB grinned again.

"I'd better go and see what's going on," he said. "Excuse me."

As JB went out to see the dogs, Aunt Harri smiled at the girls.

"I'll just pop out to the van to get Tal's bag of jelly beans," she said.

The girls looked at each other in alarm as Aunt Harri walked out.

"We can't give Tal that bag," said Kirsty with a groan. "The jelly beans are bound to taste awful."

"How can we stop Aunt Harri from handing it over?" asked Rachel.

"We've got something else to worry about first," said Kirsty, pointing at the door. "Look."

Three pairs of extra-big feet were stomping into the animal shelter. The girls looked up from the feet, over three pairs of knobbly green knees and into the faces of three scowling goblins.

"Oh no," said Rachel. "What are goblins doing here?"

The goblins didn't notice the girls. The

goblin with the biggest feet picked up the giant jar of jelly beans from the counter and took off the lid. Then he poured every single jelly bean out of the jar into a large sack.

"That's stealing," Kirsty said, horrified.

Rachel dashed towards the goblins.

"Stop!" she cried. "Give me that sack!"

She tried to grab the sack, but the goblins snatched it out of her way.

"These jelly beans are for Jack Frost," shouted the biggest-footed goblin. "Back to the Ice Castle!"

There was a flash of blue magic, and then the goblins and the jelly beans disappeared.

Jelly Bean Castle

Lisa zoomed out of Kirsty's rucksack, waving her wand. There was a burst of glittering fairy dust, and then the girls felt as if the air around them was shimmering. A wave of multi-coloured sparkles wrapped around them, followed by another ... and another. They lifted

Rachel and Kirsty into the air, rolling around them until they were spinning in a sea of colour.

"I feel dizzy!" said Kirsty, giggling.

"I don't think I know which is the right way up any more," said Rachel.

They felt their shoulders tingling, and

then beautiful fairy wings appeared.

"We're shrinking to fairy size," said
Kirsty in delight.

"We have to follow the goblins," said
Lisa. "This is the quickest way."

The waves rolled higher, surrounding
them with colour. Then there was a
whooshing sound, and they felt as if they
were being sucked towards the waves.
Seconds later, they had left the animal
shelter far behind. They twisted and
turned through a whirl of colours, until at
last they dropped down on to a soft, grey
cloud, and everything stopped spinning.

"Where are we?" asked Rachel, pushing
the fluffy cloud out of her way so that
she could sit up.

Kirsty fluttered her wings and looked
around. Everything looked dull and fuzzy.

"Are we in Fairyland?" she asked, feeling doubtful.

"Yes," said Lisa. "It's OK – we're above the Ice Castle. I brought us to a snow cloud in case Jack Frost was watching."

The three fairies fluttered to the edge of the cloud. Peeping over, they saw Jack Frost's castle below. The towers were white with a layer of frost, and the gardens stretched out towards the forest.

"Oh my goodness, look at the moat," said Rachel. "It's like a ball pool!"

Jack Frost's moat was always frozen over, but today there wasn't a glimmer of ice to be seen. Instead, the moat was completely covered with colourful jelly beans, which were piled high and hid every speck of ice.

"Look up there, behind the castle," Kirsty exclaimed.

A hill of jelly beans was looming over the moat. Jack Frost was standing on top of it, looking down at several goblins who were lying at the bottom, giggling. Other goblins were sliding down the hill on tin trays, sending jelly beans flying into the air as they landed in the moat.

"There must be thousands of jelly beans here," said Rachel in astonishment.

"Yes, and I know exactly how Jack Frost has done it," said Lisa. "Look what's in his hand." Rachel and Kirsty saw a tiny

sweet glowing in the
Ice Lord's hand.
They guessed at
once that it was
Lisa's magical
jelly bean.

"We have to
get that magical
sweet back," said
Kirsty. "But how?"

"Let's go down there and watch Jack
Frost and the goblins," said Rachel.
"Hopefully we'll spot a chance to get it
back. Come on."

She, Kirsty and Lisa swooped down
to the garden, fluttering out of sight
behind the Jack Frost-shaped hedges.
They perched on the tiny branches. From
where they were standing, they could

hear Jack Frost yelling at the goblins.

"Why are you being so slow, you nincompoops?" he shouted. "Stop jelly-bean surfing and sort every single jelly bean into flavours – now!"

The Ice Lord slid down the hill and started striding around the moat with his hands clasped behind his back. He glared at the goblins as they got down on their hands and knees.

"Work faster," he growled, throwing a strawberry-flavoured jelly bean into the air and catching it in his mouth.

As he turned away, a goblin with a tuft of fluffy hair threw a strawberry jelly bean into his mouth too. Jack Frost walked on, and every time he threw a jelly bean into his mouth, the goblins did the same. Then one of them missed and

the jelly bean hit him in the eye.

"YOWCH!" he squawked.

Jack Frost whirled around and glared at the goblin. He saw the other goblins gobbling up the jelly beans and his eyes bulged angrily. His shoulders shook. His ears twitched.

"They're mine, not yours," he shrieked, pointing a bony finger at the goblins.

"B-b-but they're so yummy," wailed a tall goblin.

Jack Frost snatched a yellow jelly bean out of the goblin's hand and ate it.

"Leave the jelly beans alone!" he shouted. "Every single one belongs in my mouth."

A Sweet Storm

Jack Frost turned and scrambled back up the jelly-bean hill. The goblins carried on sorting the jelly beans, grumbling in louder and louder voices.

"Who wants these disgusting fruity flavours anyway?"

"I'd rather have frosty fungus flavour. Yummy!"

"Or morning moss. Scrummy!"

Rachel and Kirsty stared at the mounds of pink strawberry and purple grape jelly beans. They looked delicious.

"Look," said Kirsty, noticing something behind the pink jelly beans. "Isn't that the sack of jelly beans that the goblins stole from the animal shelter?"

Suddenly, an idea popped into her head. She remembered how dizzy she had felt when Lisa's magic took them from the animal shelter.

"Maybe we can make Jack Frost so dizzy that we will be able to take the jelly bean back," she said. "Lisa, could you make jelly beans swirl around him? All the colours might be enough to make him feel wobbly."

Lisa looked at the sack, too, and nodded thoughfully.

"We can use those jelly beans," she said. "We just have to get them above

Jack Frost's head."

The three fairies fluttered down behind
the pink jelly beans and hovered around
the sack. They each held on to the edge
of the sack and then Lisa looked at
Rachel and Kirsty.

"Ready?" she said. "One ... two ...
three ... fly!"

Together, they rose up into the air,
carrying the sack with them. The
goblins saw them and squawked
in alarm, but the sack was already

out of their reach.

"We have to get to the top of the jelly-bean hill," said Lisa.

The sack was heavy, and it took all their strength to flutter up to where Jack Frost was standing. The magical sweet was held clutched in his hand, and it seemed to be glowing more brightly than ever. Jack Frost glared at them and narrowed his eyes.

"He's seen us," said Rachel.

"That's OK," said Lisa in a brave voice.

"He doesn't know about our plan."

Jack Frost watched them coming with his arms folded across his chest, and sneered as they hovered above his head.

"You can't stop me," he said, cackling. "I'm going to eat all the jelly beans here and in the human world. I've got the magical jelly bean, and there's nothing you can do about it. Go ahead and drop your jelly beans on my head. I'll just eat them."

"We'll see about that," said Lisa. "On the count of three – one ... two ... three ... pour!"

They tipped the sack of jelly beans over Jack Frost's head, and Lisa waved her wand as the jelly beans poured down. They started to swirl around Jack Frost like a mini tornado, faster and faster, until

he was almost hidden in the rainbow of
jelly-bean colours.

"Stop it!" Jack Frost yelled in
frustration, waving his arms around like
windmills. "I don't like it."

"Faster!" said Lisa, and the sweet
tornado sped up.

Jack Frost clutched his head with his

hands, and his legs began to tremble.

"I'm dizzy!" he wailed.

"That's what we've been waiting for," said Kirsty. "Hopefully he'll be so dizzy that we'll be able to take the magical jelly bean from him."

"I'll do it," said Rachel. "Here goes!"

She took a deep breath and zoomed into the jelly-bean tornado. Kirsty and Lisa watched from the outside. Rachel's hand had almost touched the magical jelly bean when Jack Frost wobbled, and ... *BONK!* He fell down on to his bottom.

"WHOA!" he wailed, as he rolled down the jelly-bean hill.

His arms and legs flailed, and he turned over and over, upside down and back to front. Rachel flew over him, whizzing left and right, trying to reach the jelly bean that was clutched in his hand.

"Clear off!" he yelled, blowing an enormous raspberry at her as he tumbled.

"You can do it, Rachel!" cried Kirsty, crossing her fingers.

Foul Flavours

Jack Frost tumbled over a patch of green jelly beans and his fingers unclenched. The magical jelly bean flew out of his hand and went spinning into the air.

"Catch it, you fools!" Jack Frost roared at his goblins.

Jabbering and squealing, the goblins scrambled over the jelly beans, reaching their arms up into the air. Lisa zoomed after the magical sweet too, swerving to avoid the jumping goblins as they tried to stop her.

"Look!" said Kirsty from behind the goblins, in her loudest voice. "A frosty fungus jelly bean!"

Straight away, the goblins spun around and dashed towards Kirsty, licking their lips and drooling. As they stampeded towards Kirsty and away from the magical jelly bean, Lisa caught it in her outstretched hands. It shrank to fairy size at once.

"Yes!" cried Rachel, cheering.

Kirsty fluttered into the air, and the goblins howled. Jack Frost roared and

stamped his feet in fury.

"I want the magical jelly bean!" he bellowed. "Give it back. I want all the jelly beans in the world!"

"You couldn't possibly eat all the jelly beans in the world," said Kirsty.

"Oh yes, I could," said Jack Frost in a sulky voice. "And I'll prove it."

He started to shove jelly beans into

his mouth. The goblins watched, licking their lips, as Jack Frost began to munch his way through the jelly-bean hill. At first he ate quickly, chewing as fast as he could ram sweets into his mouth. But then Kirsty noticed something strange.

"All of a sudden, Jack Frost doesn't look quite so blue," she said.

"He's turning ... green!" said Rachel, gasping.

Jack Frost chewed slower and slower, until his mouth hung open and jelly beans spilled out of it.

He clutched his tummy.

"I don't feel very well," he said.

"I'm not surprised," said Rachel, fluttering towards him. "Nobody is supposed to eat that many jelly beans on their own. Why don't you share them with the goblins?"

"Good idea," said one of the goblins.

"What a wise fairy," said another.

Jack Frost scowled, and then let out a loud burp and groaned.

"All right, all right," he said finally, in a grumpy voice.

The goblins whooped and cheered, and then they raised their arms above their heads and dived headfirst into the jelly-bean hill. Lisa waved her wand again, and more jelly beans rained down on the group of goblins.

"Frosty fungus and morning moss flavour," said Lisa with a smile.

"I think these jelly beans are going to keep them happy for a long time," said Rachel, smiling.

"I hope so," said Lisa. "Now, I'm going to take you both back to the animal shelter. I think you have a fun job waiting for you there!"

53

She raised her wand above her head, and a shower of silvery fairy dust burst from it like a fountain. The silver floated down and landed upon the fairies, making their hair and wings glitter. It even dusted their eyelashes, so that everything they looked at seemed to be glimmering. Then the silvery sparkles faded, and they were once again standing next to the reception desk of the animal shelter. They were human again, and Lisa was fluttering beside them. Not a single second had passed in the human world since they left.

The girls looked around and saw that the giant jar was still empty.

"Quick, Lisa, the jelly-bean jar!" Kirsty exclaimed.

With a flick of her wand, Lisa filled the giant jar to the brim.

"Thank you, my friends," she said, smiling at them. "I'm so happy to have my magical jelly bean back. I can't wait to show the other Candy Land Fairies. You have made all the difference."

"We love being able to help," said Rachel.

"I'll see you at the Harvest Feast," said the little fairy. "I can't wait to play party games with you, and let you taste all the amazing sweets that we have grown."

She waved, and then disappeared back to Fairyland in a flurry of magical sparkles.

A Reward for Kindness

As Lisa's last sparkles disappeared, the
door of the animal shelter opened and
Aunt Harri came back in. She was
carrying the special Candy Land's
Helping Hands bag of jelly beans, and
had a big smile on her face.

"Here's Tal's prize," she said, her eyes
shining with excitement. "You should

take it, girls. I'd like you to be the ones
to present it to Tal."

Rachel and Kirsty held the bag
between them, and gazed down at the
pile of gleaming, colourful jelly beans.
They shared a secret smile, thinking
about how Lisa had been inside that bag

just a short time ago.

"They look delicious," said Kirsty.

"And now we know that they're going to taste delicious, too," said Rachel, smiling with relief.

Just then, they heard happy barking, and two golden retrievers bounded in. They ran up to the girls, wagging their tails. Rachel laughed and patted them.

"You two remind me of my dog, Buttons," she said.

"They're great, aren't they?" said the boy who had followed them in.

The two dogs turned and weaved around the boy's legs, leaning against him and panting happily.

"They're saying thank you because I just took them

for a walk," he said, smiling and gently rubbing their ears.

Rachel and Kirsty exchanged a knowing smile. They knew that this had to be Tal.

"What are their names?" Kirsty asked.

"Candy and Sweetie," the boy replied. "And I'm Tal."

Before the girls could introduce themselves, the door at the back of the shelter opened, and JB came in with another man and a woman.

"Ah, I see you've found Tal," he said. "These are Mark and Niki, and they work here at the shelter too. When I told them why you were here, they were keen to come along too."

Tal looked around with a confused expression. He couldn't understand why

everyone was smiling at him. Then
Rachel and Kirsty stepped forward.

"Tal, everyone here would like to
reward you for your kindness and
helpfulness," said Kirsty.

"Your friends told the people at Candy

Land about all the volunteering work you do here," said Rachel. "You're super kind to all the animals, and you walk them every day, no matter what the weather's like or how tired you are."

"My Aunt Harri asked us to give you this," said Kirsty. "She works at Candy Land, and you have won their Helping Hands award. Congratulations, Tal!"

Together, Rachel and Kirsty handed the big bag of sweets to Tal. His mouth fell open and his cheeks went pink. JB, Niki, Mark and Aunt Harri clapped.

"Thank you," Tal said. "I can't believe it! Jelly beans are my absolute favourite sweets in the world."

"You deserve it," said Rachel, giving Tal a big smile.

Tal grinned, and then put the jelly beans on the desk.

"Before I get my treat, my friends deserve theirs," he said.

He reached down behind the desk and pulled out a tin of doggie treats. Soon, Candy and Sweetie were crunching bone-shaped biscuits and wagging their tails even harder than before. Then Tal offered his jelly beans around to everyone before taking one himself.

"I got a pink one," said Kirsty, popping it into her mouth. "Mmm, strawberry flavour. Delicious!"

"Mine's grape," said Rachel, who had chosen a purple one. "These are yummy."

"Much better than morning moss or frosty fungus," Kirsty added in a whisper.

Rachel looked around. Everyone else was chatting to Tal. She could talk to Kirsty without being overheard.

"I keep thinking about the jelly beans that are growing in the orchard at the

Fairyland Sweet Factory," she said. "Do you remember how bright and plump and tasty they looked?"

Kirsty nodded.

"I expect that the fairies are busy picking the sweets for their Harvest Feast tomorrow," she said. "Oh, Rachel, I hope

that we can help to get the last magical sweet back from Jack Frost before then."

"We have to," said Rachel, feeling determined. "We can't let Jack Frost spoil the fairies' special day. Don't worry. The Harvest Feast is going to be amazing, and I can't wait to be part of it!"

The End

Now it's time for Kirsty and Rachel to help ...

Shelley the Sherbet Fairy

Read on for a sneak peek ...

Rachel Walker was sitting at the bottom of the stairs in her best friend Kirsty Tate's house, doing up her party shoes.

"It's kind of your schoolfriend to invite me to her birthday party," said Rachel.

"Anna knows how excited I am to have you staying with me for a whole week," Kirsty said, smiling. "She's looking forward to meeting you."

Rachel jumped to her feet and smoothed down her party dress.

"I'm ready," she said. "Let's go."

Kirsty put their presents for Anna into a bag and then opened the front door.

To her surprise, she saw her Aunt Harri standing there.

"Oh!" said Aunt Harri. "That's lucky – I was just about to knock. Goodness me, you two look smart."

"We're on our way to my friend Anna Goldman's birthday party," Kirsty explained.

"I know," said Aunt Harri. "Actually, I'm here to give you a lift to the party. You see, Anna has won a Candy Land Helping Hands award, and I was hoping that you would present it to her."

Kirsty clapped her hands together in delight.

"This will be a perfect birthday surprise for Anna," she said. "She has raised lots of money for the Wetherbury Children's Hospital."

Aunt Harri worked at the Candy

Land sweet factory. She was in charge of organising the Helping Hands awards, which were special parcels of sweets for local children who did helpful things around the community. Kirsty and Rachel had been helping her to present the awards all week.

Kirsty and Rachel said goodbye to Mr and Mrs Tate, and then jumped into Aunt Harri's Candy Land van. It didn't take long to reach the Wetherbury village hall.

"Wow, the village hall looks amazing," said Kirsty.

Rachel looked up too. Colourful balloons were tied to the hall railings and there were more around the doorway. A huge banner above the door said HAPPY BIRTHDAY, ANNA!

"I'm good friends with Anna's mum," said Aunt Harri. "We got up early this morning and came here to do the decorations. I'm still shaking the sparkles out of my hair!"

The girls laughed as they got out of the van. Aunt Harri stayed in her seat.

"Aren't you coming in?" Kirsty asked.

"I'll be back soon," said Aunt Harri. "First I'm going to Candy Land to pick up Anna's cake. Her mum told me that her favourite sweet is sherbet, so her Helping Hands award is a special sherbet birthday cake. I'll bring it here for the end of the party, and you can both help me to surprise Anna."

As soon as the girls heard the word 'sherbet', they exchanged a worried glance. Luckily, Aunt Harri didn't seem to notice. The girls waved goodbye as she drove off. Then they walked up the path towards the hall, carrying the present bag between them.

"Oh dear, I'd forgotten how much Anna likes sherbet," said Kirsty in a low voice. "I hope her cake won't be ruined by Jack Frost and his naughty goblins."

Sweets had been going wrong ever since Jack Frost and his goblins had stolen the magical objects from the Candy Land Fairies. Rachel and Kirsty had helped their fairy friends to get three of the objects back, but there was still one missing.

Rachel looked down at the bag of presents and stopped in her tracks.

"Kirsty," she said in an urgent whisper. "Look!"

The bag of birthday presents was glowing as if a ray of sunshine was trapped inside. Feeling bubbly with excitement, Rachel and Kirsty peered inside. To their delight, they saw Shelley the Sherbet Fairy sitting on top of a sparkly birthday bow.

Shelley looked summery in her sunshine-yellow dress, with a beautiful pink rose in her brown hair. She fluttered out of the bag and flitted back and forth between the girls.

"Rachel and Kirsty, I have to get my magical sherbet straw back from Jack Frost," she said in an urgent voice. "The Harvest Feast is today. Please, will you help me?"

"We'll do everything we can to help," said Rachel.

On the first day of Rachel's visit to Wetherbury, Monica the Marshmallow Fairy had whisked the girls away to the Sweet Factory in Fairyland. She had introduced them to Gabby the Bubble

Gum Fairy, Lisa the Jelly Bean Fairy and Shelley the Sherbet Fairy.

The Candy Land Fairies had just invited the girls to the Harvest Feast, when there was a commotion in the orchard. Jack Frost and his goblins were shaking sweets off the trees. In the confusion, they stole four sparkly magical sweets from the Candy Land Fairies. Jack Frost wanted lots and lots of sweets for the new sweet shop at his Ice Castle, but instead of selling sweets, he was going to eat them all himself.

Without their special sweets, the fairies couldn't make sure that all sweets in Fairyland and the human world were sweet and delicious. Rachel and Kirsty had promised to help get them all back. They had found three, so now they just had to help Shelley get her magical sherbet straw back.

Just then, the door of the village hall started to open.

Read **Shelley the Sherbet Fairy** to find out
what adventures are in store for Kirsty and Rachel!

Calling all parents, carers and teachers!
The Rainbow Magic fairies are here to help
your child enter the magical world of reading.
Whatever reading stage they are at, there's
a Rainbow Magic book for everyone!
Here is Lydia the Reading Fairy's guide to
supporting your child's journey at all levels.